Jenny's Magic Wand

by Helen and Bill Hermann
photographs by Don Perdue

A GROLIER COMPANY

Franklin Watts

New York London Toronto Sydney

1988

Library of Congress Cataloging-in-Publication Data
Hermann, Helen.
Jenny's magic wand / by Helen and Bill Hermann ;
photographs by Don Perdue.
    p.   cm.
Summary: Having attended a school only for blind
children, Jenny worries about starting regular classes in a
public school until the day she proves she is "just one of the
kids."
    ISBN 0-531-10292-0
    [1. Blind—Fiction.   2. Physically handicapped—Fic-
tion.   3. Mainstreaming in education—Fiction.]   I. Hermann, Bill.   II. Perdue, Don, ill.   III. Title.
PZ7.H43164Je 1988
[E]—dc 19   87-23743   CIP   AC

The publishers are grateful to the teachers and students of the New York Institute for Special Education, and especially to Judy Strauss-Schwartz, Coordinator of Development and Community Relations, for their valuable time and for all the kindness and help they provided.

The publishers wish to express their appreciation to Claire Sullivan and the Lighthouse (the New York Association for the Blind) for their advice and help in the preparation of the manuscript.

Thanks, also, to Rita Golden Gelman.

My name is Jenny. I was born blind, so my fingertips help me look and see. I have had a lot of help, especially from Cheryl, who taught me how to use a cane so that I could move around safely.

I'll tell you more about that, and about all kinds of things that happened to me, and even about how I became a hero.

My mother found out about a school for blind children. She telephoned the teacher who told her that the school helped to prepare blind children for regular classes in public schools.

On the first day, my mother took me to school. "The room is filled with color and light," she told me. What she said gave me a warm and happy feeling.

My teacher, Ms. Taylor, gave me a doll carriage to push around. When I ran into something, she told me what it was and where it was located.

I learned by listening, touching, smelling, and sometimes by bumping into things!

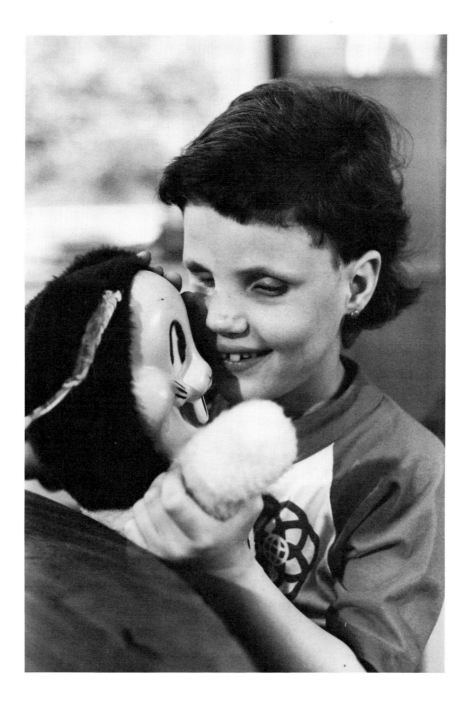

There was a toy I liked called a popcorn popper. It was a round cylinder with a handle attached. The handle was attached at the same angle that a cane held by a blind person touches the ground.

I pretended that the popcorn popper was my cane. When I pushed it, it made a popping noise. I really liked that, and the noise let people know that I was coming.

9

My friends and I also learned body balance. We practiced by standing on a big block of wood that was curved at the bottom. This made it rock. The top had strips of carpet so our feet could grasp the surface as we rocked.

The first time I did it I was scared. Ms. Taylor held me lightly at the waist. "Jenny, hold both arms straight out from your sides and rock gently back and forth."

Little by little I got used to it. After a week it became my favorite game.

"Now," said Ms. Taylor, "you can play with some toys. It will help you learn to use the smaller muscles in your fingers."

I liked that too. We didn't try to build anything, but we put small puzzle parts into holes. One hand found the empty hole and the other put in the pieces. I had just enough time to put in five pieces when Ms. Taylor called us to a sing-along.

She turned on the phonograph and we heard a funny song. The singer then told us to join in. Ms. Taylor said, "Here's a song for Jenny. When we come to the name, let's all say 'Jenny,' and Jenny will stand up and take a bow."

We all liked this game. It made us feel good to hear our friends sing our names. It is a good feeling to stand up and take a bow.

One day Ms. Taylor asked us to tell each other about funny things we remembered. Erick began.

"My mother and I spent a lot of time in the kitchen. The bottom kitchen cabinets belonged to me. They were filled with wonderful things to play with: big wooden spoons, a flour sifter, measuring spoons, plastic containers, and—of course—pots and pans.

"While I banged the pots or filled the bowls with all kinds of things, my mother always told me what I was doing. She says that's how I got to be so smart."

Then Angela remembered something.

"When I first came here to school, I had a hard time getting a drink from the water fountain. I used to get so thirsty!"

"And then Ms. Taylor taught me to press the bar so that I could get the spout going. I could hear it and I would put my hand inside so that I could feel the water. Then it took a while for me to learn how to get the water without getting wet. Now I don't have to be thirsty—ever—and I can stay dry!"

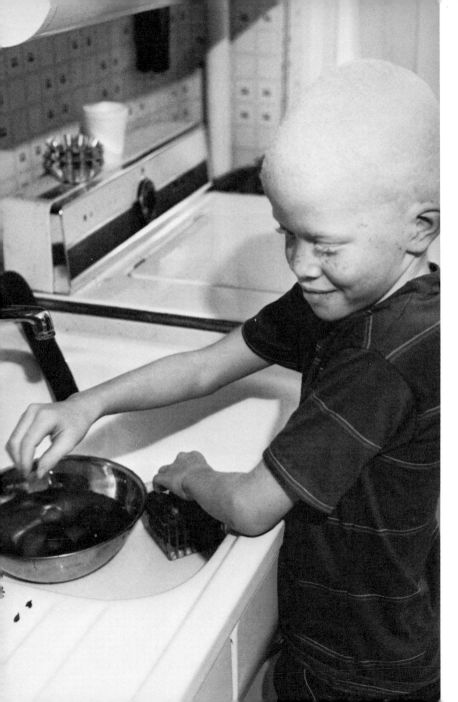

Next it was Paul's turn.

"One of the nicest things I remember is when my mother taught me how to clean strawberries. They're *so* good to eat.

"Just by feeling them I soon found out how to take the green tops off and how to rinse them in a bowl of cold water so they'd be nice and clean. Strawberries are still my favorite fruit."

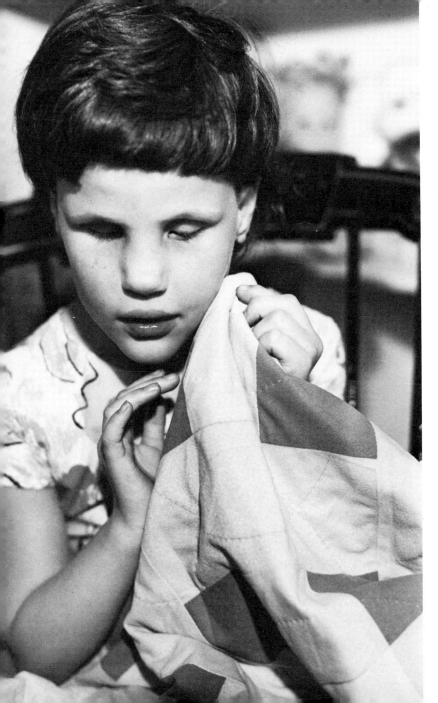

Then it was my turn.

"When I was six months old, my grandmother made me a patchwork quilt. It had furry squares and silk squares, itchy squares and bumpy squares. One square felt like sandpaper. Another was a soft, creamy velvet.

"I used to lie in my crib and rub the quilt between my fingers, moving from the soft to the scratchy to the silky. My grandma said, 'Jenny will learn the differences in texture. She will learn by touching and feeling.'"

Soon Cheryl started working with me. She's the special instructor who teaches blind people how to move around using a cane.

The cane is a light, long steel rod with a plastic tip and a rubber grip. It is very sturdy and helps me travel safely. You can carry it easily in cars, buses, and planes.

Cheryl showed me the right way to hold the cane and how to tap it back and forth, just the width of my body. In that way it will bump into things before I do.

After a lot of hard practice, I discovered that the cane could lead me through the world. I could safely go to lots of places that I had not gone before. The cane was almost like a magic wand.

One of the nicest things we learned at school was how to make lunch.

One day we learned how to make pizzas and strawberry milkshakes. First Ms. Taylor took a package of English muffins and gave one to each of us. Then she said, "I'm putting a plate with the fillings on the table. As I call out your name I will put it in front of you and you can put the fillings on your muffin."

So we piled the ingredients high on the muffins. Then Ms. Taylor put all the muffins back on the platter and put it into the microwave.

While the pizzas were cooking, we made strawberry milkshakes. Ms. Taylor gave each of us a large paper cup and added a scoop of ice cream.

"Mash it up with your spoon," she said.

As we did, she filled the cup halfway with milk and told us to stir up the mixture. Then she put everything into a blender and mixed it. Out came the best strawberry milkshake I ever tasted!

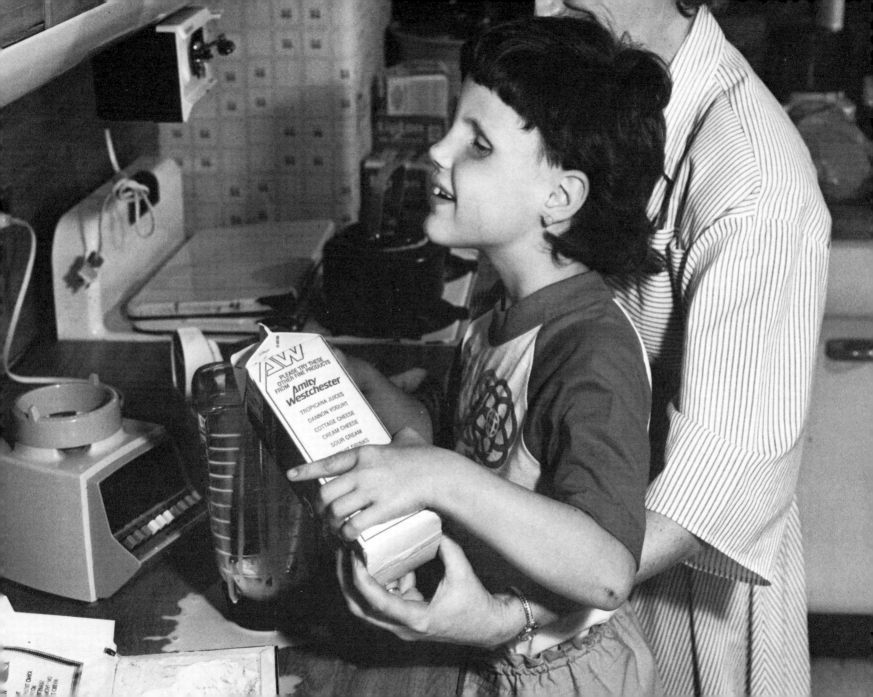

I loved my school, and the time I spent there was wonderful. We laughed a lot and helped each other.

But the idea of going to another school was scary. I spent all summer worrying about it. For the first time I would be going to school with kids who could see.

It helped that Angela, Paul, and Erick would be going there too. Angela said to me, "Don't be scared, Jenny. Remember that we learned a lot of things that those kids don't know. They need to learn about us and we need to learn about them."

Angela was right. And it was dumb for me to have worried.

On the first day the teacher and the children showed me around. When it was time for recess, I told my new friends that I would be able to find my way around the playground easily by using my cane. I used the careful sweeping and tapping motion Cheryl had taught me and I soon knew where every piece of playground equipment was. When I got to the slide I was able to climb to the top and slide right down. At the bottom a girl named Dottie said, "Jenny, you seem to see with your cane as well as I do with my eyes."

"It's just like a magic wand," I answered.

I made many friends who were very nice to me. Some of them, like Dottie, realized that with my cane and with just a little help, I could do anything they could do. Many of the other children, though, did not understand this, and they treated me specially. They were *too* nice to me.

It was not a feeling I liked. But one day something happened that changed all that.

It was the day of our Halloween party. We had made
wonderful costumes—costumes for witches, pirates, and
monsters. Mrs. Wade, our teacher, put them away in the
storeroom.

On the day of the party, Mrs. Wade opened the door to
put in one last costume. Then the bell rang for recess.
Mrs. Wade locked the door with her key.

On the playground, Mrs. Wade stood in her usual place, watching us while we played.

Soon she said, "It's time to go back."

So we went in.

She reached into her pocket for the key to the storeroom, but it wasn't there.

"Oh dear," she said. "I have mislaid the key. Please look for it on the floor around my desk and in front of the storeroom."

"We won't be able to have our costumes and we won't be able to have our Halloween party," Angela cried.

Then I got an idea. "Dottie," I said quietly, "come outside with me and my cane."

I led the way out onto the playground. Using my cane, I led her past what I knew were the monkey bars, the climbing rings, and the slide.

"Dottie, isn't this where Mrs. Wade usually stands while we play?"

"Why yes," Dottie said, "but so what?"

"Dottie, do you know what Mrs. Wade does while she stands here during recess?"

"Of course," Dottie said. "She watches us carefully."

"And she fiddles with the keys in her pocket," I said.

I got down on my knees and began to sift through the sand, feeling carefully and thinking about what my fingers were telling me.

I found the ends of three popsicle sticks, half of a toy car, the end of a comb, a quarter, a bus token, an earring and . . . the KEYS!

"Dottie," I shouted. "Come here! I've found some keys."

I walked swiftly, moving my cane before me.

I walked up to the closet and slipped the key into the hole. It turned and the door opened.

"Jenny did it!" Dottie shouted. And then she told everyone how I had found the key.

After that most of the kids understood that I wasn't helpless. They realized that I wasn't really any different from them. They saw that I could do things for myself and even for others. And that was the way I wanted it. I was just one of the kids.